P.J. Funnybunny®
and His Very Cool Birthday Party

by **Marilyn Sadler**
illustrated by **Roger Bollen**

A Random House PICTUREBACK® Shape Book

Random House 🏠 New York

Text copyright © 1996 by Marilyn Sadler
Illustrations copyright © 1996 by Roger Bollen
All rights reserved under International and Pan-American Copyright Conventions.
Published in the United States by Random House, Inc., New York, and simultaneously in Canada
by Random House of Canada Limited, Toronto.
Library of Congress Catalog Card Number: 95-69624   ISBN: 0-679-87788-6

Manufactured in the United States of America 10 9 8 7 6 5 4 3 2

One morning P. J. Funnybunny woke up with a wonderful feeling inside. Today was his birthday! "Cool!" he said.

Mrs. Funnybunny gave P. J. a big hug and a kiss.
"Today is a day that will be filled with many surprises!"
she said.

Just then there was a knock on the door. P. J. went to
answer it.

"Happy birthday!" shouted P. J.'s friends when he opened
the door. What a surprise to see all of them standing there!

P. J. was surprised to see so many presents, too.

"Now for the best surprise of all!" said Mrs. Funnybunny, with a mysterious twinkle in her eye. "Follow me."

P. J. and his friends followed Mrs. Funnybunny out to the car and piled in. What was the best surprise of all going to be? they wondered.

"I bet I know where we're going!" shouted Ritchie.
"We're going swimming!"
Ritchie couldn't wait to try out the new tall slippery slide at the lake.

"That's true," said Mrs. Funnybunny. "You'll be going swimming."

"I knew it!" said Ritchie.

But when they came to Forest Hill Lake, Mrs. Funnybunny drove right past it!

"I know where we're going!" blurted Buzz. "We're going horseback riding!" Buzz wished he had brought his new cowboy hat.

"Yes, you are going riding," said Mrs. Funnybunny. But when they drove by Mrs. Dapple's Horseback Riding Camp, Mrs. Funnybunny didn't so much as turn her head.

"I know!" Potts Pig joined in. "We're going to the ice cream shop! What's a birthday party without cake and ice cream!"

"Yes, we're certainly going to have cake and ice cream," said Mrs. Funnybunny. But when she came to Mrs. Hogg's Sweet Shoppe, she drove right past its hot-pink sign.

As they approached the Turtle Creek Boat Club, P. J. was more confused than ever.

"Mom," he said, "are you taking us on a boat ride?"

"Mmm," she answered. "You'll be doing a bit of boating."
But when Mrs. Funnybunny didn't stop at the Turtle Creek
Boat Club either, P. J. began to whine.

"Aw, come on, Mom," he cried. "Please! Tell us where
we're going!"

"Well…" Mrs. Funnybunny hinted, "at times it will be scary!"

"I know!" cried P. J. "*Attack of the Slimy Carrots* is playing at the Old Valley Cinema!"

But when Mrs. Funnybunny cruised on past *Attack of the Slimy Carrots* at the Old Valley Cinema, P. J. and his friends slumped down in their seats.

"Argh!" they groaned.

Then suddenly, everyone spied some bright lights
winking at them above the treetops. As they got closer,
a big Ferris wheel rose up before them! Next they saw
something streaking quickly by—a super-fast roller
coaster! Now everyone knew just where they were
going. They all shouted out at once:

"However did you guess?" said Mrs. Funnybunny as she drove through the gates.

And she was right. *This* was the best surprise of all.

P. J. and his friends went swimming...

horseback riding...

and boating.

They ate cake and ice cream.

And they were scared out of their wits in the
Pine Coney Island Haunted House.

Finally, as if that weren't enough, they rode the Ferris wheel *and* the roller coaster!

It was the best birthday party P. J.—or anyone else—could remember.

P. J. gave his mother a big hug and a kiss.
"Cool!" he said—and all of his friends agreed.